SIMON & SCHUSTER
BOOKS FOR YOUNG READERS
• An imprint of Simon & Schuster
Children's Publishing Division • 1230
Avenue of the Americas, New York, New
York 10020 • Copyright © 2016 by Terry
Fan and Eric Fan • All rights reserved, including the
right of reproduction in whole or in part in any form. •
SIMON & SCHUSTER BOOKS FOR YOUNG READERS is a trademark of
Simon & Schuster, Inc. • For information about special discounts for bulk
purchases, please contact Simon & Schuster Special Sales at 1-866-506-1949
or business@simonandschuster.com. • The Simon & Schuster Speakers Bureau
can bring authors to your live event. For more information or to book an
event, contact the Simon & Schuster Speakers Bureau at 1-866-248-3049 or visit
our website at www.simonspeakers.com. • Book design by Lizzy Bromley • The text
for this book is set in Adobe Garamond. • The illustrations for this book are rendered in
graphite and colored digitally. • Manufactured in China • 0317 SCP • 10
• Library of Congress Cataloging-in-Publication Data • Fan, Terry. • The Night Gardener / by Terry
Fan and Eric Fan.—1st edition. • pages cm • Summary: Everyone on Grimloch Lane enjoys the trees and
shrubs clipped into animal masterpieces after dark by the Night Gardener, but William, a lonely boy, spots
the artist, follows him, and helps with his special work. • ISBN 978-1-4814-3978-7 (hardcover : alk. paper)
• ISBN 978-1-4814-3979-4 (eBook) • [1. Topiary work—Fiction. 2. Gardeners—Fiction.] I. Fan, Eric. II. Title.
• PZ7.F36Nig 2016 • [E]—dc23 • 2014041306

FOR MOM AND DAD
—T. F. & E. F.

The Night Gardener

Terry Fan & Eric Fan

Simon & Schuster Books for Young Readers
NEW YORK   LONDON   TORONTO   SYDNEY   NEW DELHI

William looked out his window
to find a commotion on the street.
He quickly dressed, ran downstairs,
and raced out the door to discover . . .

The wise owl had appeared overnight, as if by magic.
William spent the whole day staring at it in wonder,

and he continued to stare until it
became too dark to see.

That night he went to sleep
with a sense of excitement.

The following morning,

William was not disappointed.

Each day William discovered a new topiary.
Next was a friendly rabbit,

followed by a pretty parakeet . . .

and then a playful elephant.

With each new sculpture, the crowds grew and grew.

Something was happening on Grimloch Lane.

Something good.

The next day, William dashed out of his home

and followed the crowds, only to find . . .

the most magnificent masterpiece yet!

Festivities continued
long after the sun had set.

As William was about
to head home,

he spotted someone unfamiliar.

Could it be?

The gentleman turned to William.
"There are so many trees in this park.
I could use a little help."
It *was* the Night Gardener!

Under the light of
a full moon,

they worked deep
into the night.

William awoke to the sound of happy families walking by,

and a gift from the Night Gardener.

The whole town had come out to admire the
Night Gardener's—and William's—hard work.

Over time the leaves changed . . .

and then fell,

until there was no evidence
that the Night Gardener
had ever been to
Grimloch Lane.

But the people of the small town
were never the same.

And neither was William.